IMAGINARY MENAGERIE

A BOOK OF CURIOUS CREATURES

Poems by Julie Larios

Paintings by Julie Paschkis

HARCOURT, INC.   ORLANDO   AUSTIN   NEW YORK   SAN DIEGO   LONDON

Para todos los buquis de la familia Larios
— J. L.

For Owen and Adam Turner
— J. P.

Library of Congress Cataloging-in-Publication Data
Larios, Julie Hofstrand, 1949–
Imaginary menagerie: a book of curious creatures/Julie Larios;
[illustrated by] Julie Paschkis.
p. cm.
1. Animals, Mythical—Juvenile poetry. 2. Children's poetry, American.
I. Paschkis, Julie. II. Title.
PS3562.A7233163 2008
811'.54—dc22   2006037442
ISBN 978-0-15-206325-2

First edition
H G F E D C B A

Manufactured in China

The illustrations in this book were done in gouache on Arches paper.
The display type was set in Post Antiqua.
The text type was set in Tiepolo.
Color separations by Bright Arts Ltd., Hong Kong
Manufactured by South China Printing Company, Ltd., China
Production supervision by Pascha Gerlinger
Designed by Linda Lockowitz

Contents

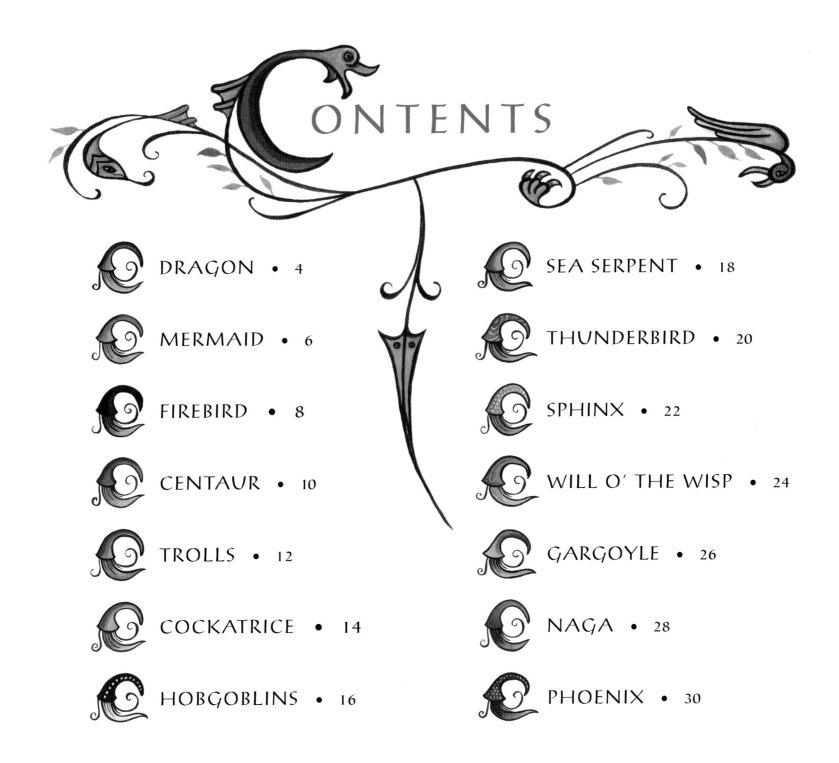

RAGON

The air around me
burns bright as the sun.
I tell wild rivers
which way to run.
I'm arrow tailed,
fish scaled,
a luck bringer.
When I fly,
it's a flame song the world sings.
But you can ride safely
between my wings.

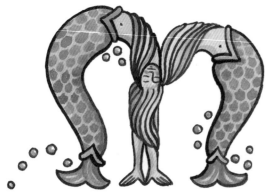

MERMAID

Listen to the waves
break on the shore—
half song, half roar.
Listen to the beach
answer back—
half cry, half laugh.
Underneath it all,
you might hear a splash,
you might hear a call,
or you might hear a sigh,
long and low.
What does she say,
part woman, part fish?

I wish . . . I wish . . .

FIREBIRD

Who will bring me golden apples?

calls the firebird

from her silver tree.

Who will sing me a golden song?

All day she waits

in the tsar's garden.

Who will set me free? Who?

If given a feather

bright as heaven,

would you?

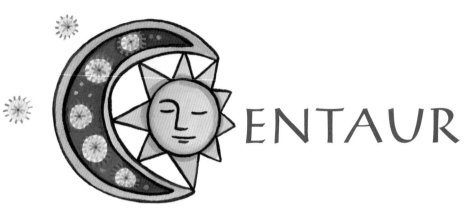 # CENTAUR

Can he be half gallop, half walk?

Half dream, half real?

Half neigh, half talk?

Can he be half man, half horse?

The answer is no.

And yes, of course.

TROLLS

With rushes and mud,
with mud and sedge,
they build their beds
under the bridge.
Don't ever cross it
if the sun has set.
Troll arms will grab you
and put you in a pot—
in with the turnips
and the dung and the spuds,
in with the beetles
and thistles from the ditch . . .
You'll be a troll's supper
under the bridge.

COCKATRICE

I'm a snake-tailed rooster,
I'm a rooster-headed snake.
All it takes
to turn you to stone
is one look from me.
Ki-ki-ri-ki-ri!
Should I crow or should I hiss?
S-ss-sss-ssss-sssssssssssssss . . .

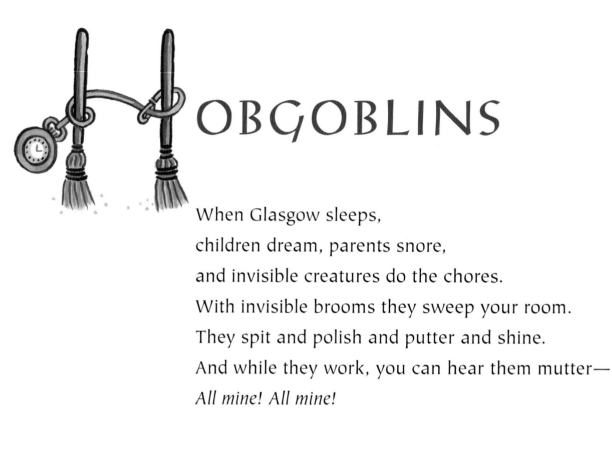

HOBGOBLINS

When Glasgow sleeps,
children dream, parents snore,
and invisible creatures do the chores.
With invisible brooms they sweep your room.
They spit and polish and putter and shine.
And while they work, you can hear them mutter—
All mine! All mine!

SEA SERPENT

Sailors call me Monster of the Deep,
Ocean Emperor,
Sea Master.

Tonight when you sleep,
why don't you swim with me
through water?

I'll call you Friend,
Fellow Traveler,
Ship Swallower.

THUNDERBIRD

Do you hear the thunder crack?

Do you hear it rumble?

Here he comes!

His wings

beat the old drums.

Cedar scented,

he carries the wind

in his bent beak.

Rainmaker.

Whale hunter.

Great Tlingit chief.

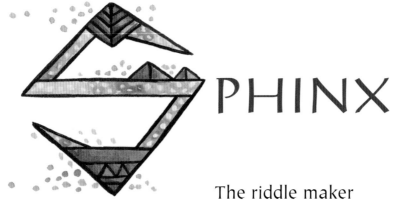

SPHINX

The riddle maker
is silent now.

So the sand asks
How?
Why?
When?

But the cat-man sleeps.
He never even stirs.
No one can answer
the sand.

ILL O' THE WISP

She's a trick of light
as dusk turns to dark.
See how she floats
toward the sad swamp trees?
You'll be lost if you follow
and your feet touch water.
Try not to listen when she cries
Catch me!

25

GARGOYLE

How can a beast speak
with a stone tongue,
with a stone throat?
My mouth is a rainspout.
I screech. I shout.
How can a beast fly
with stone wings?
I fly when the bells ring
and the hunchback is home.
Does a stone beast sleep
in a stone nest?
I am on guard.
I never rest.

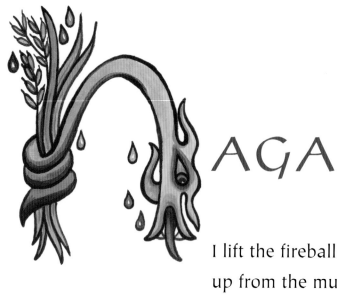

NAGA

I lift the fireballs
up from the mud
of the Mekong River
into the sky.
Who am I?
I am the naga of seven heads.
I water the grain.
When sun shines through me
after the rain,
I paint the temple
with seven colors.

PHOENIX

Rising
from the ashes of her nest,
away she flies.
She is a bird that never dies.
Singer
and shape-changer,
she is a strange one:
Now a crane, now a drake,
now a turtle, now a snake,
now a swallow,
now a swan—
she burns and is reborn.
And then she's gone.

More about the IMAGINARY MENAGERIE

DRAGON
The word *dragon*, traced back to ancient Greek, means "seeing one." Although dragons are usually thought to be enormous, in some traditions they're depicted as small as rabbits or butterflies.

MERMAID
Many cultures believed that mermaids could foretell the future or, like their cousins the selkies and the Finfolk, that they tried to lure humans into the sea.

FIREBIRD
Russian folklore holds that a firebird's feathers are magic. In Iran the huma is a similar bird from the Persian storytelling tradition. In Mexico the mythical plumed serpent Quetzlcoatl has feathers that shine as if on fire.

CENTAUR
Ancient Greeks said the centaurs' mother was a rain cloud, and their father was the sun. Centaurs represented the divided nature of man—sometimes wild and warlike, sometimes civilized.

TROLLS
Tales of these devious creatures come from Scandinavia, the Orkney Islands, and the Shetland Islands. Trolls were often accused of stealing human babies and substituting their own changelings to be raised by unsuspecting parents.

COCKATRICE
Also known as a *basilisk* (from the Greek, meaning "little king"), this beast is mentioned several times in the Old Testament.

Legend has it that the only way to kill a cockatrice is to make it look into a mirror; it turns itself instantly to stone through its own gaze.

HOBGOBLINS
Along with their imaginary relatives, the bugbears and boggarts, hobgoblins originated in the folklore of the British Isles. People have long told stories about moody and unpredictable hobgoblins to scare naughty children into behaving well.

SEA SERPENT
Modern sightings of supposed sea monsters continue to be reported. Over the years, sailors from Maine to Brazil have blamed these beasts for the unexplainable disappearance of countless ships at sea.

THUNDERBIRD
The thunderbird, a familiar icon in the tribal art of the Pacific Northwest, exists in the storytelling traditions of many other native people across North America, including the Sioux Nation of the Great Plains and the Passamaquoddy of Maine.

SPHINX
A common figure in Egyptian, Greek, and Southeast Asian mythology, this human-headed lion almost always guarded access to something sacred, such as a temple or a funerary site.

WILL O' THE WISP
Throughout the British Isles, these fairy-like beings were said to carry lanterns, also known as "fool's fire," through bogs and marshes, luring travelers who had lost their way in the dark.

GARGOYLE
Like the sphinx, gargoyles were thought to guard sacred sites and to ward off demons and evil spirits. Familiar figures on the cathedrals of medieval Europe, these grotesque creatures can be traced as far back as ancient Egypt.

NAGA
Naga water deities continue to be celebrated in the Hindu and Buddhist cultures of Southeast Asia, India, and Malaysia. Not always seen as benevolent, nagas are sometimes blamed for droughts and floods.

PHOENIX
First detailed in the Egyptian *Book of the Dead*, the burning bird is a familiar mythological figure. In Christian tradition, the bird's ability to be reborn becomes the crucial detail. Ancient Greek mythology describes the phoenix singing so beautifully that the sun stops in its path across the sky to listen to her song.